Giggle, Giggle, Quack

ARTIST'S NOTE

For this book I did brush drawings using Winsor & Newton lamp black watercolor on tracing paper. I then had the drawings photocopied onto one-ply Strathmore kid finish watercolor paper and applied watercolor washes to the black drawings. The advantage to this method is that I can get as many copies on the watercolor paper as I want, and I can experiment with the color, choosing the finishes that I like the best.

SIMON AND SCHUSTER

First published in Great Britain in 2003 by Simon & Schuster UK Ltd
Africa House, 64-78 Kingsway, London WC2B 6AH

Originally published in 2002 by Atheneum Books for Young Readers
an imprint of Simon & Schuster Children's Publishing Division, New York

This edition published in 2004 by Pocket Books

Text copyright © 2002 Doreen Cronin
Illustrations copyright © 2002 Betsy Lewin

The right of Doreen Cronin and Betsy Lewin to be identified as the author and illustrator of this
work has been asserted by them in accordance with the Copyright, Designs and Patents Act, 1988

Book designed by Anahid Hamparian
The text for this book is set in Filosofia Bold

All rights reserved, including the right of reproduction in whole or in part in any form

A CIP catalogue record for this book is available from the British Library upon request

ISBN 0-7434-9009-6
Printed in China
3 5 7 9 10 8 6 4 2

For Andrew
—D. C.
For Rosanne Lauer
—B. L.

Giggle, Giggle, Quack

by Doreen Cronin   pictures by Betsy Lewin

SIMON AND SCHUSTER
London   New York   Sydney

Farmer Brown was going on holiday.
He left his brother, Bob, in charge of
the animals.

"I wrote everything down for you.
Just follow my instructions and
everything will be fine. But keep
an eye on Duck. He's trouble."

Farmer Brown thought he heard giggles and snickers as he drove away, but he couldn't be sure.

Bob gave Duck a good long stare
and went inside.
He read the first note:

Tuesday night
is pizza night
(not the frozen
Kind!).
The hens prefer
anchovies.

Giggle, giggle, cluck.

Twenty-nine minutes later
there was hot pizza in the barn.

Bob checked on the animals
before he went to bed.
Everything was just fine.

Wednesday is bath day for the pigs.
Wash them with my favourite bubble bath and dry them off with my good towels.
Remember, they have very sensitive skin.

Giggle, giggle, oink.

Bob had all the pigs washed in no time.

Farmer Brown phoned home on
Wednesday night to check in.
"Did you feed the animals as
I wrote in the note?" he asked.

"Done," replied Bob, counting seven empty pizza boxes.

"Did you see my note about the pigs?"
"All taken care of," said Bob proudly.

"Are you keeping a very close eye on
Duck?" he asked.

Bob gave Duck a good long stare.
Duck was too busy sharpening his
pencil to notice.

"Just keep him in the house," ordered Farmer Brown. "He's a bad influence on the cows."

Giggle, giggle, moo, giggle, oink, giggle, quack.

Giggle, giggle, moo.

Bob was in the kitchen, popping corn. Just as the animals settled in to watch THE SOUND OF MOOSIC, the phone rang.

The only thing
Farmer Brown
heard on the
other end was:

"Giggle, giggle,
quack, giggle,
moo, giggle,
oink . . ."

UH-OH.

"DUCK!"

screamed Farmer Brown.